IF **Not**
FOR THE
Cat

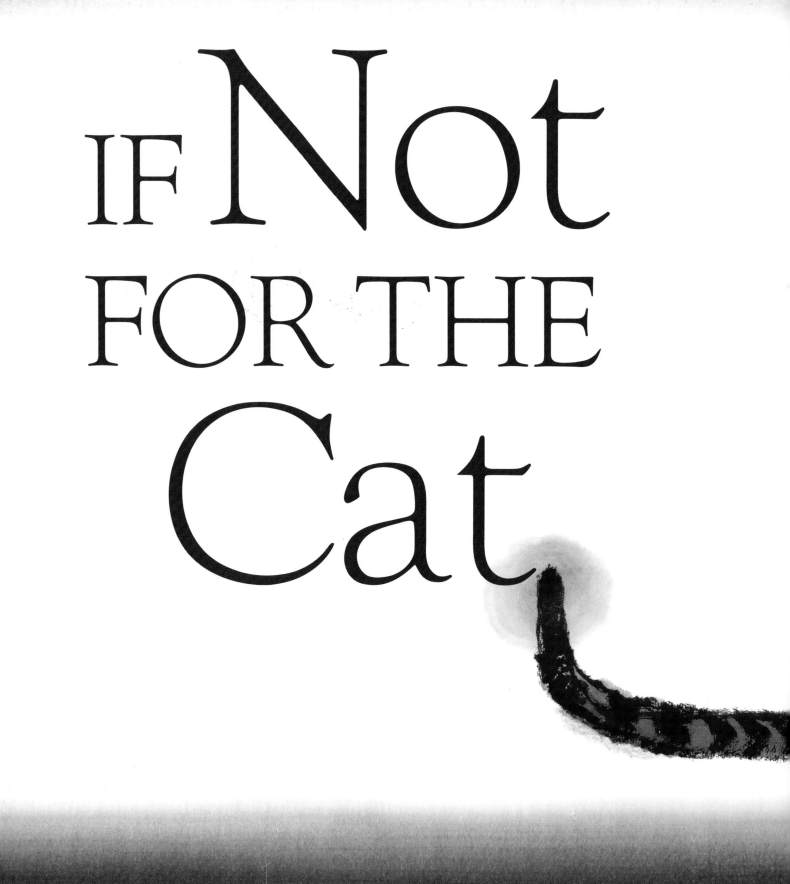

HAIKU BY
Jack Prelutsky

PAINTINGS BY
Ted Rand

Greenwillow Books
An Imprint of HarperCollins*Publishers*

If Not for the Cat

Text copyright © 2004 by Jack Prelutsky

Illustrations copyright © 2004 by Ted Rand

www.harperchildrens.com

The art is a mix of sumi brush drawings in India ink, traditional watercolors, chalk, spatter, and printmaking techniques. It was done on rag stock watercolor paper and rice paper.

The text type is 32-point OPTIElizabeth.

Library of Congress Cataloging-in-Publication Data

Prelutsky, Jack.

If not for the cat / haiku by Jack Prelutsky ; paintings by Ted Rand.

 p. cm.

"Greenwillow Books."

Summary: Haiku describe a variety of animals.

ISBN 0-06-059677-5 (trade). ISBN 0-06-059678-3 (lib. bdg.)

1. Animals—Juvenile poetry. 2. Children's poetry, American. 3. Haiku, American.

[1. Animals—Poetry. 2. American poetry. 3. Haiku, American.] I. Rand, Ted, ill. II. Title.

PS3566.R36I35 2004 811'.54—dc22 2003017064

First Edition 10 9 8 7 6 5

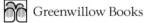 Greenwillow Books

For Mary Chalker
—J.P.

With love, to Gloria
—T.R.

If not for the cat,
And the scarcity of cheese,
I could be content.

I, the hoverer,
Sip the nasturtium's nectar
And sing with my wings.

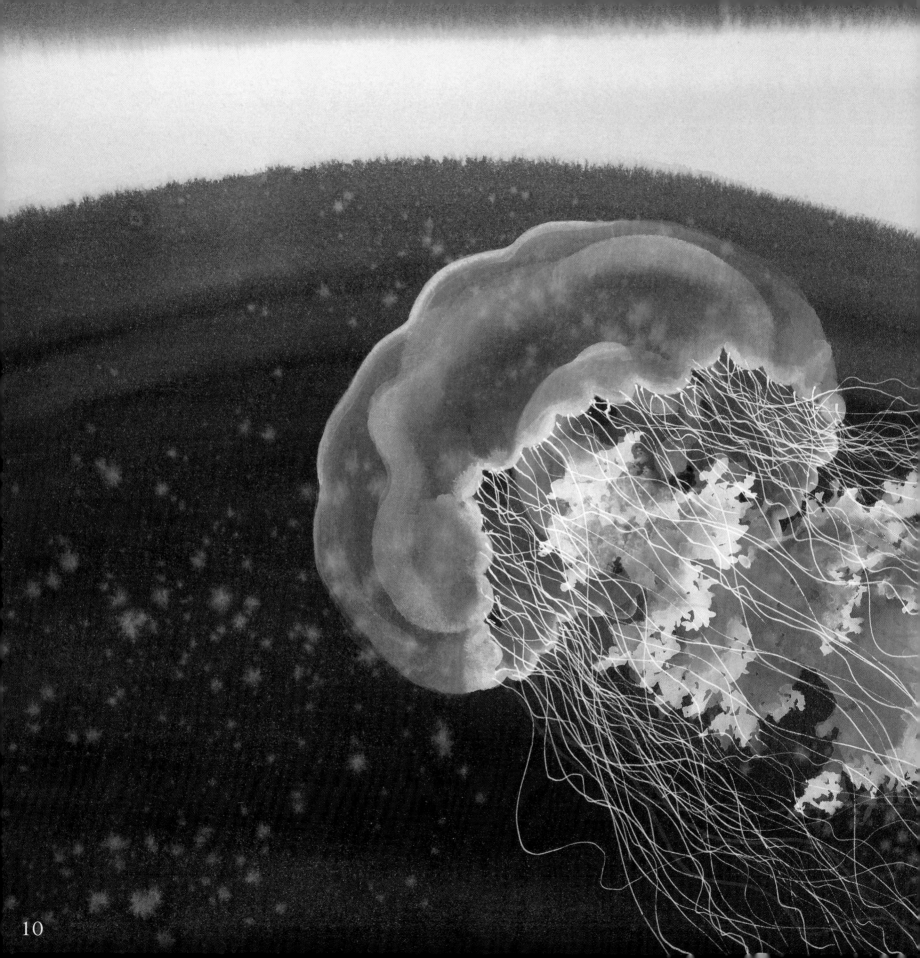

Boneless, translucent,
We undulate, undulate,
Gelatinously.

I am slow I am.

Slowest of the slow I am.

In my tree I am.

We are wrinkled hulks
With astonishing noses.
Our ears block the sun.

How foolish I am.
Why am I drawn to the flame
Which extinguishes?

Raucously we caw.
Your straw men do not fool us.
We burgle your corn.

I snack on my back,
Crack my dinner on my chest—
Bliss in the water.

Don't think about it—
Just leave the vicinity
If you hear my tail.

Gaudily feathered,
With nothing at all to say,
I can't stop talking.

We are we are we
Are we are we are we are
Many in our hill.

I spend all my time
Picking ants up with my tongue.
It's a busy life.

Safe inside my pouch
Sleeps the future of my kind—
Delicate and frail.

I have no hatchet
And yet I fell a forest.
My teeth are my tools.

From nests in the clouds
We survey our dominion
With telescope eyes.

When I raise my tail,
Expressing my displeasure,
Even wolves make tracks.

Wingless we went in,
But we emerged as fliers—
And oh, such colors!

Who is Who